Zoom Squirrel?

Zing Squirrel?

Flappy Squirrel?

Norman?

Wonder Squirrel?

Mo Squirrel?

Wink Squirrel?

Klink Squirrel?

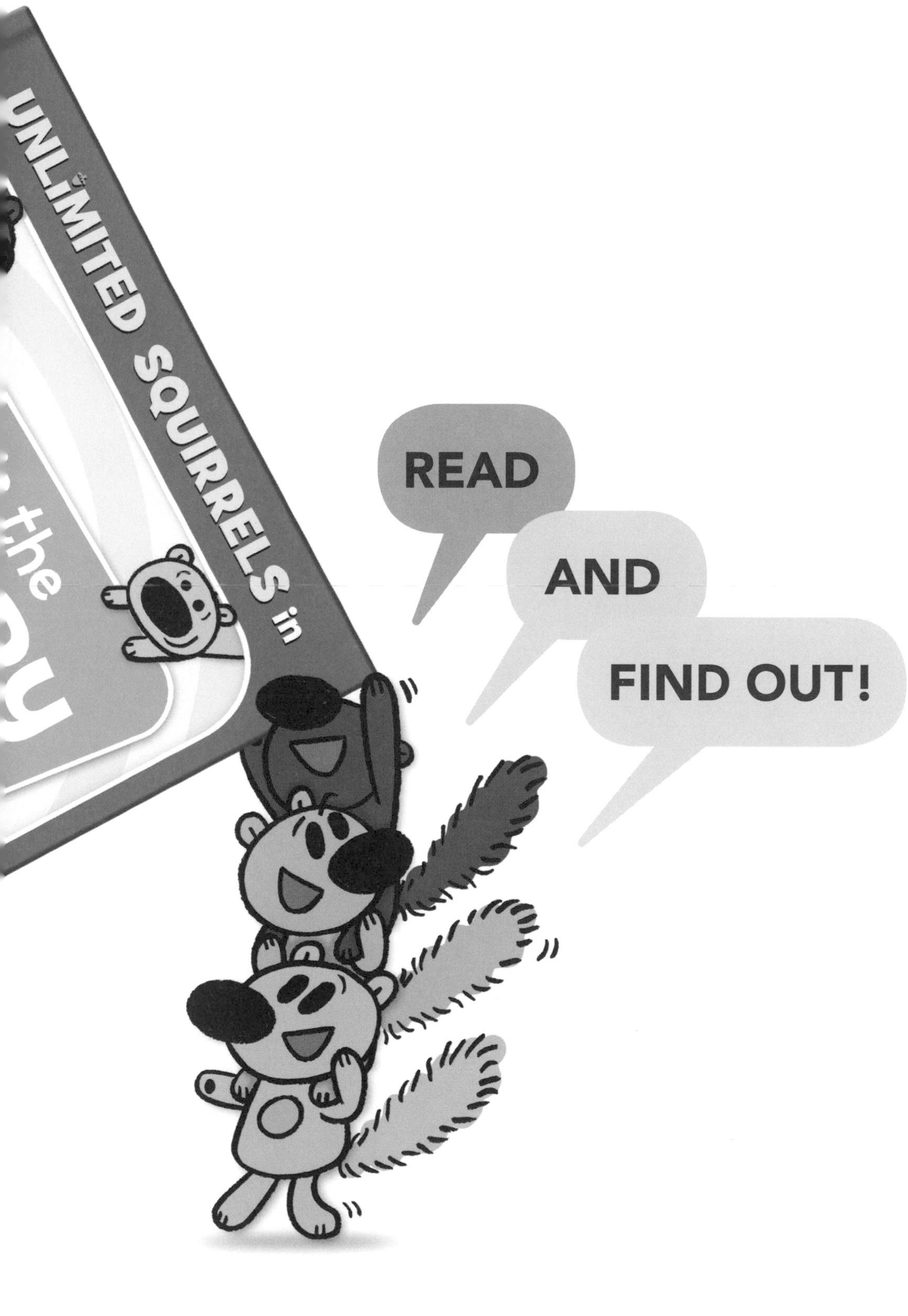
UNLIMITED SQUIRRELS in
READ
AND
FIND OUT!

TABLE of CONTENTS

Look for the **EMOTE-ACORNS** in this story.

They pop up when the Squirrels have **BIG** feelings!

SURPRISED

FRUSTRATED

EXCITED

DETERMINED

HAPPY

PROUD

CONFUSED

SAD

FUNNY

The BIG Story!

> WHO IS THE MYSTERY READER?

By Mo Willems

I do **not** know what that sign says.

Why not **read** it?

The **mask**!

The **underpants**!

It's the—

MYSTERY READER!

The **sign!**

It says **something!**

But **WHAT**?

I will **READ** the sign!

So brave!

So cool!

My hero!

Such a reader!

...OP!

STOP!

Stop **making sounds** and start **reading**, please.

I like to **sound out** the letters.

It helps with some words!

WON DER FUL!

LET ME TRY!

STOP!

The sign says "**stop**"!

Great work, Zoom Squirrel!

Squirrel **pride.**

Excuse me...

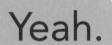

Thanks to the **Mystery Reader**.

Yeah.

Where is the Mystery Reader?

So fast.

So **mysterious**.

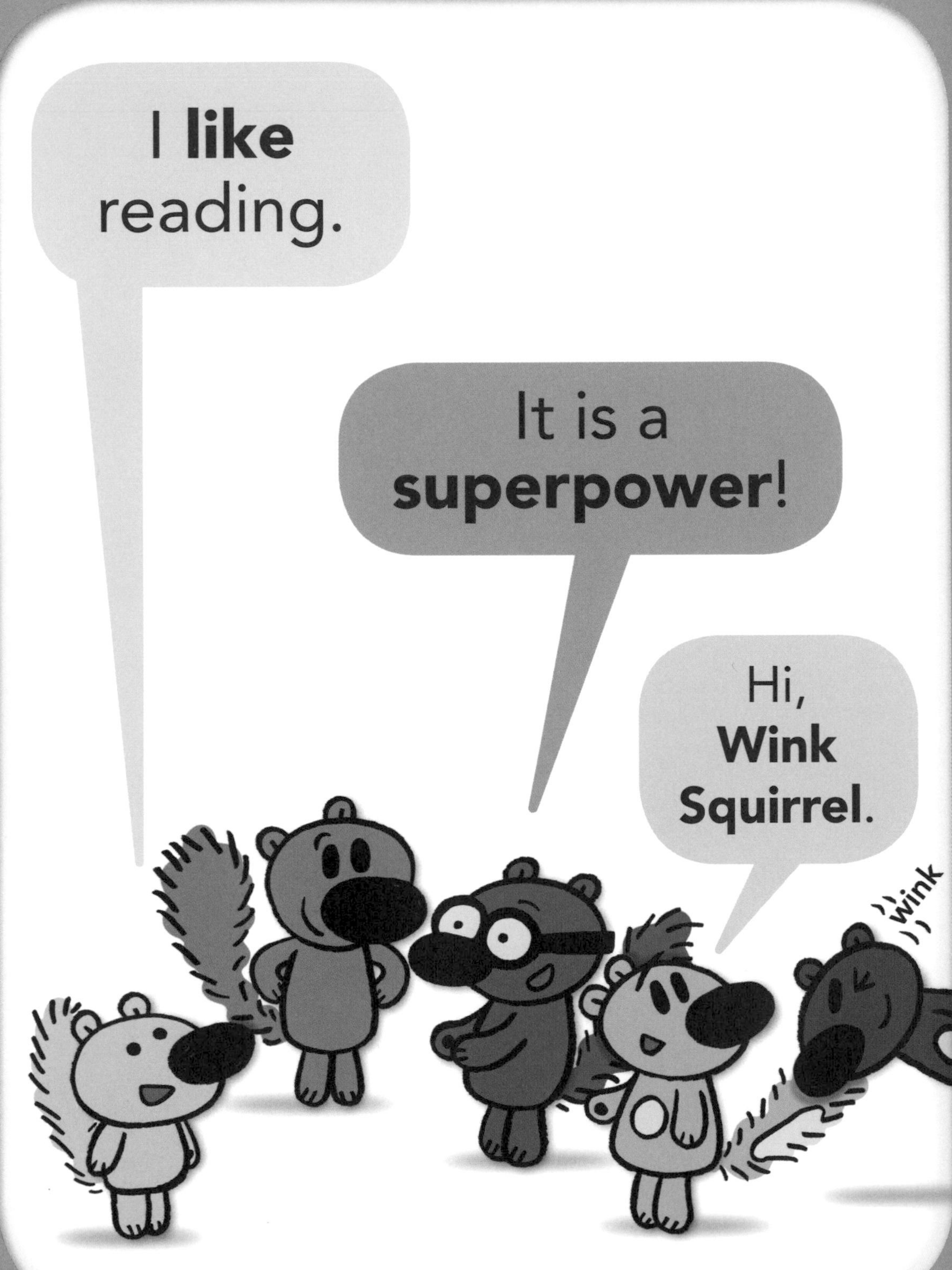
I **like** reading.
It is a **superpower**!
Hi, **Wink Squirrel**.
wink

The Mystery Reader's **card** is a **clue**.

I will **try to read** the card!

I...

am...

the...

34

I thought the Mystery Reader was **taller**.

And had **more teeth**.

This **is** a mystery.

The **MYSTERY READER** is back!

NEW MYSTERY READER!

I love **Mystery Readers**!

You can be a Mystery Reader, too!

Mask and **underpants** are optional!

It's ACORN-Y JOKE TIME!

100% CORNY!

Hey-Corn! How is the **alphabet** like a **post office**?

Hi-Corn! I do not know. How **is** the alphabet like a post office?

They are both **FULL OF LETTERS**!

That joke **delivered**!

Look! Head in the clouds!
Tail on the ground!

It's
WONDER SQUIRREL!

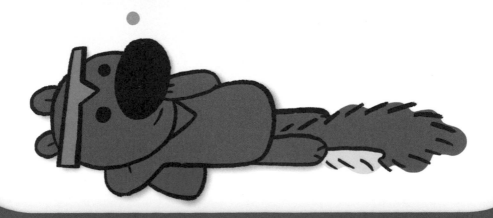

I am wondering: What did the **very first writing look like**?

THE BOOK OF WONDERS!

What **power!**

What **strength!**

What **binding!**

THE WRITE STUFF

The oldest known writing is called **cuneiform**. It was created over **5,000 years ago.**

Cuneiform was written by wedging a **special stick** into wet clay. Once the clay dried, there was no erasing it!

At first, some modern experts thought cuneiform was writing. Some thought it was art. Others thought it could be **bird footprints**!

Wowie!

Now we know that cuneiform was often used to record **history** and **sales**—like the paper receipts we have today.

Zowie!

The ancient **Egyptians** used pictures to show sounds and words. These are called **hieroglyphs**. The ancient **Maya** also wrote in hieroglyphs.

Many of the **26 letters** in the English alphabet come from **Egyptian hieroglyphs**. They look a lot different now!

The letter **A** started out as the hieroglyph for **ox**. Over time, the ox shape changed as it passed to other languages.

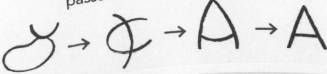

Let's **turn** the page!

There are between **750** and **1,000** hieroglyphs for most of Egyptian history.

There are over **900** Maya hieroglyphs.

I want to learn **more**.*

*To learn more, go to unlimitedsquirrels.com!

WRITE ON

People wrote on **stone**, **clay**, **wax**, **bone**, and **papyrus** in ancient times.

The **Inca** civilization used bundles of **knotted ropes** to keep records.

Paper was invented in **China** about **2,000 years ago**.

Paper can be made from many things, like **tree bark**, **cactus**, **old underwear**, and even **animal poop!**

Zowie!

Wowie!

WHO IS THE MYSTERY WRITER?

Many writing mysteries remain! Like . . .

WHO INVENTED THE SCROLL?
We don't know! Some scrolls have survived for thousands of years buried in **Egyptian tombs**.

WHO INVENTED THE BOOK?
We don't know! We do know that the oldest complete books we have today are over **1,600 years old**.

WHO INVENTED INK?
We don't know! We do know that ancient Egyptians made ink from **soot** (burned material) mixed with **plant gum** and **water**.

Now I am **full—**

Maybe YOU will solve one of these mysteries!

Cool!

WONDER

FULL!

It's ACORN-Y JOKE TIME!

100% CORNY!

Hi-Corn! What is the best way to **start reading**?

Hey-Corn! I have no idea! What **is** the best way to start reading?

I like being **in** a book! It is **fun** to be read!

But **how** did we get into this book?

Well...

SPACE SQUIRRELS

By Mo Squirrel

"A writer named Mo Squirrel tried to come up with **ideas** for a story."

"After Mo Squirrel thought for a long time, an idea **started to take shape.**"

"Mo Squirrel told the idea to two pals, **Agent Squirrel** and **Editor Squirrel**."

"The Squirrels **asked questions** that helped to make the story **better**."

"Mo Squirrel **wrote**!"

"Mo Squirrel **drew**!"

Middle

"Mo Squirrel **re-wrote**!"

"Mo Squirrel **re-drew**!"

"Until Mo Squirrel thought the story was **done**!"

"But, it wasn't."

With more work,
it could be **better**.

"Mo Squirrel **re-re-wrote!**"

"Mo Squirrel **re-re-drew!**"

"Until, finally, it was really **done**."

"Then a **book printer** printed the story."

It's ACORN-Y JOKE TIME!

92% CORNY!

Hey-Corn! How is **this book** like **this ball**?

Hi-Corn! You got me! How **is** this book like this ball?

THE TALE END!

I love this book about **MYSTERY READERS!**

A BIG SQUIRRELLY THANK-YOU TO OUR EXPERTS!

Niv Allon, assistant curator, Department of Egyptian Art, the Metropolitan Museum of Art

Keith Houston, author of *The Book: A Cover-to-Cover Exploration of the Most Powerful Object of Our Time*

David Stuart, author of *The Order of Days: Unlocking the Secrets of the Ancient Maya*, Schele Professor of Mesoamerican Art and Writing, and director, the Mesoamerican Center, the University of Texas at Austin

Printed in Malaysia • Reinforced binding • This book is set in Avenir LT Pro/Monotype; and Billy/Fontspring
First Edition, October 2019 • 10 9 8 7 6 5 4 3 2 1 • FAC-029191-19228

Visit hyperionbooksforchildren.com
and pigeonpresents.com

Library of Congress Cataloging-in-Publication Data

Names: Willems, Mo, author, illustrator.
Title: Who is the Mystery Reader? / by Mo Willems.
Description: New York : Hyperion Books for Children, 2019. • Series: Unlimited Squirrels • Summary: As Zoom Squirrel and friends try to identify the Mystery Reader, they learn about books, how they are written, and how to read—while sharing a-corny jokes.
Identifiers: LCCN 2019002890 • ISBN 9781368046862 (paper over board)
Subjects: CYAC: Books and reading—Fiction. • Squirrels—Fiction. • Acorns—Fiction. • Jokes—Fiction. • Mystery and detective stories. • Humorous stories.
Classification: LCC PZ7.W65535 Whs 2019 • DDC [E]—dc23
LC record available at https://lccn.loc.gov/2019002890